A CHRISTMAS BRIDE FOR THE COWBOY

KRINGLE CHRISTMAS TREE RANCH

MIA BRODY

This is a work of fiction. Names, characters, places, and incidents either are the product of the author's imagination or are used fictitiously. Any resemblance to actual persons, living or dead, events, or locales is entirely coincidental.

Copyright © 2022 by Mia Brody

All rights reserved. No part of this book may be reproduced or used in any manner without written permission of the author except for the use of quotations in a book review.

1
CASSIE

West Kringle is not a true Kringle. At least, not in spirit. I don't even know why the grumpy cowboy still works at the Kringle Christmas Tree Ranch that his parents built. All he does is stomp around here and boss employees around.

There's no Christmas cheer to be had around this cowboy. He spends every holiday season avoiding the crowds that flock to his family's farm. He doesn't help out Ledger and Micah who give customers tours of the place. He doesn't show up at the gift shop and help his mom bag and ship the orders. When he does deign to join the weekly family dinner, he barely says a word to any of us.

No, he's too busy fussing over the trees and

harvesting them to mingle with his family. Or he was. His father's recent health scare changed everything.

Now, the annoying man is everywhere I turn. He's usually scowling at me too. Always looking like he walked out of a hot cowboy calendar while he ducks his head under the brim of his Stetson.

He's outside my workshop right now, banging on the door with his big fist and yelling at me to open up. I know it's him because he's announced it like three times and he's not going away. Why can't he take a hint?

"It's too early for this," I mutter as I pull my face up from my workshop table. It releases me with a sticky popping noise which means I must have fallen asleep working late again last night. I scrub at my stiff cheek and hope there's no paint on it.

Christmas is my busiest season. It's when Cassie's Creations are most in demand. Not only do I sell my toys at the Kringle gift shop but on their website too. Plus, there are the organizations that serve foster kids who can always use extra donations this time of year.

I yell that I'll be there in a second and reach for my cardigan, slinging it around my curvy body. This workshop used to be an old barn that I'd work out of. Then West caught on and within just a couple of weeks, he had it transformed into a real woodshop for me, complete with a heating system.

I tried to thank him but he just growled at me, "No sense in you freezing your fingers off."

So, yeah, that's West. He's my brother's best friend and the man that infuriates me even when he's doing something nice for me.

I nearly trip over Snowball as I make my way toward the door of my shop. She's the white kitty I adopted from the shelter earlier this year. She hisses at me, but I don't take it personally. She's hissed at every single person I've brought her around.

"What do you want?" I demand when I open the door and see him standing there. It's not even seven in the morning and he has the audacity to look hot in his black t-shirt and tight blue jeans.

I think his mouth quirks, but it's gone too soon for me to tell. I wish he were easier to read. I've never been able to figure this man out or why he drives me so crazy. The Kringles adopted me when I was fifteen. Micah had just turned eighteen so he couldn't legally be adopted. But they took us both in and raised us alongside West, their biological son.

"Coffee," he grunts the word. He's a total caveman around me most of the time. But he'll talk to Micah. I've heard them chatter a hundred miles a minute when they're talking about a car they're repairing or planning one of their stupid fishing trips with Ledger.

I step back and let him inside the workshop.

The moment he crosses the threshold, he yanks the Stetson off his head. His thick wavy brown hair is starting to streak with silver already. Micah and Ledger tease him about it. They call him an old man. Secretly, I think it looks incredibly sexy. It even matches his beard that's peppered with gray too.

His brown gaze rakes over the shop, and I don't like the way I feel so exposed and vulnerable with him looking at my creations. There's a reason I don't let most people in here. This is my heart, and I don't want to share it with anyone.

To distract myself, I thread my way around the seating area in my workshop and toward the coffee machine I keep in the back. I don't get many visitors other than mom and dad. But I like them to be comfortable when they do visit.

Snowball meows at West. It's the first time she's ever made any noise other than a hiss. But why on earth did she choose to bestow that gift to West?

He chuckles when she brushes up against him. I can't say I blame the girl. I'd like to rub up on him too. He kneels next to her and pulls up his sleeves, revealing the ink from his tattoos. There's the pink one from his mom's cancer diagnosis three years ago and the trout that's a tribute to his late grandfather who took him fishing every summer. Plus, a few more, but I haven't seen them. I never lie awake at night wondering what they all are or if he has tattoos anywhere else.

"Such a pretty girl," he murmurs in a soothing tone. He picks her up gently and she comes willingly, snuggling against his chest. Why am I not surprised? My grumpy cat likes the grumpy cowboy.

"You didn't come all this way for a cup of my coffee," I tell him as I start the old machine that hisses and hums to life, enveloping my space in the sweet scent of warmed caffeine.

My words have him pulling his attention from inspecting my workspace to inspecting me. His gaze narrows as he takes in my candy cane striped mini dress and matching white leggings. I bought the dress that hugs my curvy figure from Mallory at Sew Cute. "What in the hell are you wearing?"

I wrap my arms around myself and fight the urge to tug the material down my thighs. He's seen me in less clothes when we'd go down to the river. There's no reason for him to make a big deal out of this. "What do you care?"

"It makes me hungry." Something flickers across his face. Shock, surprise, maybe horror. I don't know. It's too hard to read West and I've spent years making myself crazy as I've tried.

"You've never had a sweet tooth." He never touches dessert, never indulges in anything really. He's wound too tight for that, always has a need to be in control. I'd love to be the one person that slips under his defenses. That makes him lose his control.

An image of the two of us together floats into my mind. Him above me, panting and sweaty. Saying the dirtiest things in that raspy voice of his. Telling me that he owns me now, that he'll never let me go. It's silly and I don't let myself indulge in those fantasies. Ever. That would be a one-way ticket to heartbreak city.

"Not why I'm here," he grinds out and shakes his head. He lowers Snowball to the ground who makes a mournful sound at the loss of contact with him. Then he starts for the door like he might leave again.

"Did all the Whos finally realize it was you?" I call out in a teasing tone. It's no secret that everyone thinks he resembles a certain green monster who destroys the holidays for those who do find joy in them.

He pauses and turns back to me, a half-smile playing at his lips. This has got to be a new record of near smiles for me. "It was that damn Cindy Lou."

"She spoils everything. Is that why you're here? Are you trying to get new toys to clear your name?"

"Not exactly." He pulls off his Stetson again and spins it in his hands, the way he does whenever he's not sure what to do next. I've spent a lifetime studying this man, learning his habits and quirks.

"I could use a bride for Christmas," he finally announces.

"I don't make those kinds of toys here," I quip at him even as my chest feels too tight. West is getting married. I didn't even know he was dating. He's never brought a woman home to meet his parents and that's just not how things are done in Courage County. So, who is the mystery woman and why am I already jealous of her?

"I need a real woman. Someone to help me out." He's not looking at me anymore.

Finally, I understand what he's saying. He doesn't have a woman. He's looking for someone to help him. I don't think I want to know the task he has in mind.

"Maisy might be willing to do it," I answer. She and I recently became friends. She moved back home to Courage to care for her adoptive brothers after her parents passed away this summer.

He snorts. "Striker would have me strung up by my thumbs before noon."

OK, so that is true. Striker runs the Cardinal Ranch and he's fiercely protective of anything that's his. Including Maisy. He kidnapped her one night and they fell in love. Not long after that, they were married.

"I had someone else in mind for the job." His voice has that dark, raspy note that makes me want to close my eyes and listen to it again and again, like a beloved song.

"What do you need her for anyway?" West has always been handsome and even though I try to ignore their looks, I see the way other women pay attention to him. It doesn't matter if they're locals who have known him all his life or women visiting the farm for holiday cheer.

My stomach hurts when I see their looks because I know that some woman will eventually snag his attention then he'll be hers. I'll have to sit across from her at family dinners and pretend that I don't think about her husband.

The coffee pot makes a noise to indicate it's finished brewing. I pull two chipped mugs from the cabinet. They have holiday puns on them because Dad loves puns and he's always giving me gifts with them.

I pour West his coffee and pass it to him, careful not to touch his fingers. I'm always worried that my face will give me away. Mom says my eyes tell the truth and West is the one person I can't afford to tell the truth to.

He takes a long sip of his coffee and I watch his throat work. "Mom wants Dad to sit out of everything this year, so it looks like I'll be putting on the big red suit."

An important part of the Christmas festivities every year is the Santa's workshop event that Dad and Mom put on here. He dresses up as Santa and she's Mrs. Claus. They hand out gifts to all the kids in town and donate groceries to needy parents. Their goal is to make sure every family in Courage County has a beautiful Christmas day and I love them for it. They aren't just interested in Christmas as a business. It's a way of life for them and that means giving back to those less fortunate.

Still, I can't help the giggle that manages to escape when I imagine West in the big red suit, trying to smile down at the babies and take pictures with the sugar-hyped children who come to sit on his lap. "You're going to pretend to be jolly this year?"

"Oh, it gets better," he drawls. "You're going to be Mrs. Claus."

2
WEST

Cassie would have you believing that I'm the big green guy. The one who steals Christmas and disappoints children. But well, I've always thought they had him a little bit wrong in the movies. Maybe the fellow with the shoes too tight is just lonely. Maybe he's always been a little bit in love with someone who doesn't return his feelings.

I grew up hearing my parents talk about how they met one Christmas, and it was love at first sight. The same thing happened to me too. Only she was my best friend's little sister. She was fifteen and standing there in a pair of red tights and a short dress looking like a dream straight out of my fantasies.

I was eighteen and even if my parents hadn't

warned me away, I wouldn't have pursued her. I was best friends with Micah and besides, my folks adopted both of them. We spent every day mucking out horse stalls together and every night sharing a dinner table.

Now Christmas is a reminder that she doesn't see me as anything but her adopted brother. I can't think too much about that or my gut gets all twisted up. Mainly, I just try to avoid her and everyone else. Hell, maybe I am the green guy.

She puts a hand on her curvy hip. "I'm not playing Mrs. Claus to your Santa."

When my folks told me they wouldn't be putting on the usual Santa and Mrs. Claus costumes this year, I did the logical thing. I suggested my brother don the red suit. Ledger is the real crowd-pleaser. He already does the tours around the farm, keeping tourists and locals alike entertained as they're driven around the grounds.

But he can't do that and manage to be Santa at the same time. The next less logical solution was my brother, Micah. But he drives the tractor that attaches to the wagons. Each wagon is decorated to look like a train car. It's a Christmas train that delights our visitors year after year.

That only left yours truly for the part. I would

have balked, but I knew that would make my mom sad. If there's one thing a Southern man won't stand for, it's disappointing his mama. So, I agreed to do this for my parents and for the kids that still believe Christmas is magical.

My only problem was finding a Mrs. Claus. Until I walked by Cassie's workshop, and I realized I could get her to fill the part. She's the only one I could think of that would be available on short notice and besides, she loves the Kringle Christmas Tree Ranch.

She'd do anything for my parents as it is. Maybe not for me. But then again, that part is my fault. I've been a jack ass since the day I met her. Knew she'd never be mine so I've kept as much distance between us as I can.

"Yeah, you'll be Mrs. Claus this year," I insist. It wasn't my plan to blackmail her when I set foot in here. But now that I've entertained the possibility of her being Mrs. Claus, I can't let it go. "Otherwise, I'm telling mom what happened to her prized Mustang."

The same Mustang that sixteen-year-old Cassie borrowed at midnight and wrecked. Took it for a joyride and called her brother crying when she drove it into the ditch. By some miracle, she wasn't injured. But the same couldn't be said of the car.

Micah, Ledger, and I managed to get that thing back to the house under the cover of darkness. But the body was too badly mangled to fix. The Mustang was the joy of my mom's life but none of us would ever fess up to what happened that night.

She narrows her gaze. "We were kids. It's been ten years. She wouldn't still hold a grudge."

I'm silent because we all know the machine was like a fifth child. She babied that car and was constantly detailing it. Dad got her a new one, a midnight blue Mustang from a different decade. But it's not the same and we all know it.

"And you wouldn't tell on me anyway." Her tone is different now, not as certain. A little more desperate.

I keep silent again. I keep silent around Cassie all the time because there are things I want to tell her. Fantasies about her, filthy and depraved ones. Things a man has no business thinking about his best friend's little sister, much less whispering in her ear.

"You're trying to blackmail me. It's not going to work." She starts pacing the workshop. The little hem of her dress is swishing back and forth, rubbing across her thighs. Fuck, how is it that I'm jealous of a dress that gets to wrap around her curvy body and hug that luscious ass?

When she passes my way again, I shove my hands in my pockets to avoid the temptation to reach out and run my fingers along the soft material. I want to know if she's as firm and juicy as I'm thinking.

My favorite fantasy of us together pops into my head. The one where she's in my bed, completely at my mercy. Her pupils are blown, and her lips are swollen. She's drenched, her sexy scent filling the air. She's begging me to fill her sweet holes, to feel my cock ram deep into her.

"I'm impervious to your tricks!" She finally declares with a finger upheld.

I shrug and step toward the door. "Suit yourself."

One step, two steps. Before I can make the third, she's calling my name. Damn, it's sweet torture to hear my name on her lips and know she'll never call it in ecstasy. She'll never call it while she's writhing and moaning, her naked flesh pressed against mine.

"I'm not doing this for you." She has a defiant tilt to her chin. I want her to defy me later. I'd teach her a lesson. Keep her on edge until she was begging and pleading for her release. Only then would she get to come. Then I'd make her come again and again. Just so I could watch her curvy body shudder and shake.

"Course not," I mutter. When have I ever done anything that would make her think we're friends? It's always bugged me that I can't be the first person she calls when she has good news or the last person she wants to text at night. But hell, I made this bed. It's not right to complain that it's a cold and lonely one.

"I'm doing this because I love mom and dad," she says. "But if you ever threaten me again, I'm telling mom about the filthy magazines under the couch that you blamed on Ledger."

Shit, I forgot about that teenage lie. This is the problem with growing up with your crush. You have all the dirt on each other. "I'm telling Dad about the time you fake cried to get out of a ticket."

"I'm telling Mom about you spray painting filthy art on Old Man Teller's barn before letting his bull out of the pen."

Shit, I'm not sure about the statute of limitations on what my brothers and I did to Old Man Teller. The guy was a mean bastard to us growing up. It'd probably give him enormous satisfaction to see the three of us picking up trash on the side of the highway these days.

I hold up my hand because we aren't going to get anywhere doing this. We have a lifetime of sins and misdeeds on the other. "Let's just agree to work together in the spirit of Christmas and not because anybody is blackmailing anybody."

Her grin turns triumphant and there's a blush creeping down her neck. I want to peel that dress off and see if that flush goes all the way down. I want to know what color every inch of her skin is, know the exact shade of her nipples and the precise hue of her pussy lips.

"Deal," she announces. "Though we both know mom would have been more disappointed with you than me."

"Where's the rest of your dress?" I demand when Cassie shows up in Santa's workshop later that day in a red dress that clings to her skin like she was born in it.

What is it with Cassie wearing half-finished clothes around me? It's like waving a red flag in front of a bull. All I want to do is charge her and maul her like an animal. Pretty sure that's not the show all these decorators came to see.

We're here in the local community center, decorating it for the Santa's workshop event. Normally, my parents decorate this with the help of staff from the ranch. But they were both feeling under the weather so I told them I would head it up. They looked doubtful I could do it until I reassured them that Cassie would be there.

She rolls her eyes at me, not aware of how much it makes my hand ache to swat her ass. Damn, I'd love to turn it just as red as that dress is.

I probably have a lot of fantasies for a virgin, but they all revolve around one person. One woman that I want to discover everything with. It'd take me years to explore them with her and that's before you even get to her fantasies. *Dammit, she's not fantasizing about you.*

"Where do you want these decorations, Cassie?" Michael asks, bringing up a cardboard box for her inspection.

I see the way his gaze travels down her figure as she tells him about her plans for the community center this year.

While she talks, I catch his eye. I shoot him a glare that promises him the greatest bodily pain of his life if he ever glances in her direction again. He got the memo because he quickly excuses himself to continue unloading the decorations.

The hours pass quickly with Cassie in charge.

She's a force of nature and fearless leader. She's determined to make my parents proud with this latest workshop and it's obvious from the way she fusses over every detail that she's throwing herself into the task. Not for the first time I wonder what a Christmas season with her would be like. A real one where we're together as a couple.

"What do you think?" She asks as she steps back from the makeshift stage where Santa and Mrs. Claus are supposed to greet the eager children.

"Looks…" My voice trails off and I nod at her decorations. She added fake garland and ribbons to the fake fireplace in the corner and updated the colors on the Christmas tree. They're now silver and blue, colors that would make my dad smile.

She sighs at my lack of clear feedback and pulls out her phone, snapping several pictures. "I'll show Mom and Dad when I get home."

"I'll warm up the truck," I tell her. It's easier for me to do stuff for Cassie than it is for me to say the things I'm thinking.

She drove herself here, but there's a light accumulation of snow on the ground tonight. Since she hates to drive in the snow, I offered to take her home in my truck. I don't know which of us was more surprised when she accepted.

As soon as I'm done, I hustle back to the community center. I pause long enough to stomp my boots on the rug inside the door before I move back into the cozy auditorium. Pride fills me when I think about how this is all Cassie.

She's already back to fussing over the decorations. She's on a ladder, trying to adjust the tree topper. It makes me smile to see the way she's so obsessed with getting every detail just right for my parents.

"You about ready to go, little girl?" The term of endearment slips out before I can stop it. Dammit, this is why I keep my mouth shut around her because if I don't, she'll know the truth. See it written all over me.

She yelps in surprise and the rickety ladder she's standing on wobbles. She loses her balance and lets go of the ladder.

I don't even have time to think. My body moves on instinct, my hands going around her hips to pluck her from midair. I set her feet on the ground but still don't let go of her. The air around us is charged and crackles with every breath I take.

There's an old Christmas song on the radio. Some classic that my parents always dance to every time it plays. The only thing I can think about is how right it feels to have her in my arms. This is where she's meant to be. She couldn't see it a decade ago but maybe she can now.

For one beautiful moment, everything is exactly how it's meant to be. She's in my arms and letting me hold her close. Her vanilla scent teases me, the way it always does. Before the end of the night, I'll be pumping my cock and whispering her name into the darkness.

Then she whispers, "Thank you."

I love her. I want to tell her that. I want her to know that it's been ten fuckin' years without her and I've still saved myself like some lovesick fool. Does she ever think about me when she's touching that pretty little pussy of hers? Is it my name she calls when she comes all tangled up in her bed sheets? Fuck, please let it be me. It has to be me.

She stands on her tiptoes and presses her lips against mine. It's a gentle, tentative touch but it's just enough to short circuit every part of my brain. I cup her head in my hands, instinctively deepening the kiss. Ten years of pent-up longing are going into this kiss. Ten years of aching and loneliness and hoping each Christmas it would be the year she'd fall for me.

She's the one that finally breaks the kiss. She steps away from me, and her pupils are blown wide.

Her lips are swollen, and her nipples pebbled in that little dress. She looks like she's one second away from being fucked. The thought has me growling deep in my throat.

"We can't…I'm sorry, West." Then she turns on her heel and sprints for the door like hunting dogs are after her. My whole body is electrified, and I can't stop grinning. Cassie likes me.

Now, I just have to put my cards on the table and convince her to give me a chance.

3
CASSIE

The next morning, I'm back to working in my shop again. OK, that's a lie. I'm pretending to work in my shop. Secretly, I'm thinking about that kiss with West and how amazing it was.

"Where does this box go?" Micah asks, nudging a cardboard box filled with toys. He's always willing to help me out. Especially during this time of year when he knows I'm often overwhelmed and behind on my projects.

Snowball hisses when he steps too near her. He instantly moves around her, having gotten her little claws in his leg one too many times.

"That one is filled with toys to donate. Put it in the back of your truck," I answer, adding more red paint to the colorful block set I'm painting.

"Or add it to the sleigh," West says as he comes in. My heart flutters at the sight of him in that black plaid shirt and his tight blue jeans. He pulls off his Stetson, his gaze nearly melting me on the spot.

"You're going into town?" Micah asks as he hefts up the box with ease. At least, that's one good thing about living with my brothers and West nearby. There's no shortage of strong guys around.

"Mom asked me and Cassie to do a sleigh run for her," he answers. His tone is casual, but I hear the slight hitch in his voice. It's the only tell that he just lied to his best friend.

Micah doesn't notice though and he just carries the box outside, whistling under his breath as he goes. It's some old Frank Sinatra song that our dad loves. Just like that, my brother's warning from all those years ago comes back to me. *Don't do this. If you like him, they'll make us leave. We always have to leave.*

Even from a young age, I knew I was the problem. Families loved Micah. I was the unadoptable one, the reason we had to leave. Until we found the Kringles and suddenly, we had a home.

Micah never made me feel bad about having to leave but I could see the disappointment in his gaze every time. The way the light in his soul would dim a little more with each failed placement and my anxiety would become a little worse.

As we grew, they offered to separate us, and I knew what every social worker was telling my brother. They were telling him that he was good. He could have a family if he'd just let go of his little sister. He always refused. Even when we did get separated for a little while, he'd find his way back to me. Micah is my rock, and I can't hurt him.

Snowball approaches West with a welcoming meow, rubbing along his legs. Even I can't get the cat to greet me with anything other than a hiss.

"Mom didn't ask me to help," I tell West with my hands on my hips. I don't know why I call him out, but I do. Probably because we've always irritated each other, always gotten under the other's skin.

He picks her up and cuddles her close to his chest, like they've been best friends for years. My cat likes my crush too.

"Come with me anyway." He holds out one gloved hand, his cheeks ruddy from the winter weather. "Everyone will assume a couple of friends are spending time together."

Is it that easy to dismiss? I'm afraid my feelings for West show, that everyone knows. That scares me more than anything because the truth is, I don't want to have to leave any more than Micah does.

"We've never been friends," I answer.

He doesn't flinch. We both know we aren't friends. We're just two people thrown together in a weird set of circumstances that mean we grew up together. "Never too late to start being friendly."

Oh, the way he says the word friendly. The last thing I'm thinking about is friendship. I'm thinking about hearing his voice rumble in my ear as he calls me his good girl. I'm thinking about how it'd feel to be naked in front of a fire with only his body against mine, about the look in his eyes right before I sprinted away last night. My whole universe shifted after that kiss. It's the only thing on my brain since the moment it happened.

Before West can respond, Micah is back in the workshop.

West drops his hand, disappointment flickering in his expression. He's expecting me to reject him, to tell him no. That's the last thing I want. Besides, he said everyone would just think we're being friendly. There's no harm that can come from this.

"Let me wash up before we go," I tell him, gesturing at my messy hands that are dotted with paint. From hand-carving the heirloom wooden toys to painting them, there's not a part of the process I don't handle myself. I love that every item is handmade by me with love and care.

West's eyes light up, a sure sign that I'm probably making a mistake. I can't lead him on. It wouldn't be right. But I can enjoy a nice sleigh ride with him today. Later, I'll gently tell him this isn't going anywhere.

He hovers nearby while I wash in the big basin sink. I can hear him talking with Micah. They're casually discussing ranch business. My brother is acting totally normal, like he doesn't suspect anything is happening right under his nose.

Meanwhile, I'm back here with my face flushed and my hair a mess and all I can think about is how good it felt when West put his hands on my hips. I want him touching me in other places, murmuring again in that low, sexy voice of his.

I take a second to fix my hair and wish I could change out of the old t-shirt I'm wearing. But Micah would definitely notice that. He'd assume that my crush is back. But it never really left. I just buried it for a long time.

"You're beautiful," West says. He's watching me lock up the workshop. It's set far enough back from the rest of the ranch activities that I don't worry about human visitors. It's animals like the bears and wolves that haunt these woods that I worry about.

I can feel his gaze on me, warming me even as I stand out here in my bright red winter coat and my favorite skirt paired with blue snowflake leggings. The ones that are faded in all the right places and cling to my curvy frame.

I finish locking the door and turn to him. "That's not something you say to a friend."

He takes two steps closer, invading my space until I bump my back against the door. The sensation barely registers because all my attention is focused on the handsome cowboy. He's staring down at me with a feral hunger in his gaze. "Never said I was your friend."

My knees are weak, and my mouth is dry. "You said—"

"I said we could be friendly," he answers casually. "Seems you and I have a very different idea of what that means."

I glance around, suddenly aware that we're outside. Without thinking, I blurt out, "You can't kiss me here. Anyone could see."

He frowns and steps back. "Let's get these deliveries started."

My chest aches, thinking that I might have hurt his feelings. West is the last person I've ever wanted to hurt even if he is grumpy with me most of the time.

He helps me into the sleigh and my stomach flips. It always does when he touches me. There's a burning ache between my thighs when he settles into the seat next to me. He's pressed so closely and all I want to do is crawl into his lap and snuggle into his chest, just like Snowball did.

Once the horses have started clopping toward town, West produces a quilt. He unfolds it over my lap, pausing to tuck me in. His mother made this one. She tried to teach me to quilt but I never got into it.

Instead, I followed Dad into his woodshop. He's the one who taught me how to work with the saws and the hammers. He simplified geometry terms and algebra. He helped me to see the real-world application of those subjects when I was in his shop.

Would he be angry if he knew West kissed me and I liked it? Would he send me and Micah away? It's a chance I can't take. I've gotten shipped off from various homes for far lesser mistakes.

When he's done settling the blanket over my lap, West takes my hand and gives it a gentle squeeze.

"Why have you been so different? Did the kiss really change anything between us? We're still the same people." As soon as I blurt out the words, I wish I could cram them back inside.

"I've wanted you since we were kids," he confesses, his voice husky. "For the longest time, I didn't think you thought of me like that. Then I kissed you and I can't go back, Cassie. I can't pretend anymore."

"You like me?" The knowledge makes me feel warm all over. He likes me back. "You've always been so grouchy."

He cups my face in his hands, the intensity of what he's saying burning in those deep brown eyes of his. "Because it fuckin' hurts. It hurts to pretend year after year that I don't look at you and see my whole world."

My heart pounds at his words. This isn't like last night. I can't just sprint away. Well, not unless I wanted to jump from the sleigh, and I definitely don't want to do that. Not with West holding me so gently, so reverently.

Under the blanket, he puts his hand on my knee. I open them, giving him access to the part of me that

I want him touching. "I want to take you on a date. Lots of them."

I hesitate. I want that. I want to be with West more than anything. But it can't really be that easy, can it? I can't just decide I want to be with him. There will be consequences and I can't leave the farm.

He runs his hand higher, his fingertips brushing my thigh through the soft material of my leggings. It feels so good, so right to have his hands on me. "I know you like me back, but you're scared. We can keep it a secret. No one has to know that we're seeing each other."

The idea of being with West is all I ever wanted. Micah and I would be safe if I could be careful. No one would make us leave if they didn't know the truth. "Could we do that? Could we lie to your parents? Micah and Ledger too?"

"We're not lying. We're just protecting this thing between us while it's still fragile and new." His fingers stop just as he reaches the apex of my thighs, the place where I'm aching and wet and so in need of his touch. "Moment of truth, sweetheart. What do you want?"

Somehow, I know he's asking me about more than this, about more than just wanting his body. He wants to know if I'm willing to be brave. "Touch me."

He tucks a strand of my curly hair behind my ear before he reaches for the waistband of my skirt. It takes some shimmying, but he gets it down far enough that he can cram his big hand into my panties.

My body jolts the moment his calloused fingers connect with the soft skin of my pussy. I've never had a man touch me like this before and to get to share this with West is special.

"Fuck," he breathes as he touches my wetness, swirling his fingers through it. "You know how many nights I've fantasized about touching you here, just like this?"

"All this time I thought I was the only one who felt anything," I admit, closing my eyes to focus on the sensations he's giving me. It feels so good to have him stroking me here.

His finger finds my channel, and he pushes inside. For a moment, I let myself imagine it's his big cock. That he's pumping it into me.

He presses a kiss to my neck, whispering, "I've been stroking my cock to you for years. Always to your thick hips and these thighs, imagining how they would feel around me."

"West…" I call his name as my body tightens around his thick digit. His thumb finds my oversensitive nub and just like that, I detonate. He kisses me through the high, absorbing my cries and pleasure.

When it's over, he pulls his hand from my panties and helps me to readjust my clothes before he sucks his fingers into his mouth. He makes the loudest growling noises as he sucks them clean. I think I could come again just watching how much he enjoys the taste of my juices.

Then he kisses me again. "Have dinner at my place tonight."

I let out a soft breath, watching it hang like a puff of smoke in the air. This cowboy makes me feel brave. "Say when."

4
WEST

"It smells good in here," Cassie says as she follows me into my house. I live on the Kringle Ranch, but my place is separate. Micah and Ledger have places of their own too. Only Cassie is still at home with my parents. Probably a good thing I know they'll be waiting up for her or I'd be tempted to keep her here all night long.

"I'm making sweet potato casserole." It's her favorite. I had to go over to mom's house to grab the recipe today. When she caught me going through her recipes, she smiled.

She suspects I'm dating somebody. I don't know what she'd say if she knew it was Cassie. My parents warned me away when I was eighteen and again a few years later. In their eyes, Cassie is delicate and fragile. But she's not. She's a strong woman who's built a thriving business. She's carved out a good life for herself. She's incredible and I want to spend every day of the rest of my life showing her that.

She glances around the kitchen, like she doesn't quite know what to do with herself. She's still new to this. We both are, but I want my place to feel like her place in the coming weeks. Because by this time next year, I want her wearing my ring and carrying my baby in her belly. Just the thought fills me with anticipation.

"Let me show you around," I say casually. She's only been in here once before when I was first moving in. She helped carry some of my stuff from my parents' place to this house.

"Kitchen, obviously," I point behind myself before I walk through the dining room. It has the table and chairs I ordered from her.

"You kept this." She gives a self-conscious laugh.

Before she made wooden toys, she thought she wanted to make furniture to sell. I was her first customer. I ordered a custom dining set that I love just because she made it. She pored hours of work and dedication into these pieces.

"This is dreadful craftsmanship," she complains as she runs her fingers along the back of a chair that wobbles no matter how many times I fix it. "You should give it away or sell it on one of those marketplace apps. Get yourself something better."

"It's a custom piece," I answer. "And it's special to me."

She looks up at me, a blush stealing across her cheeks. Fuck, I want to kiss her again. I want to devour her, but I promised myself I'd take this slow. I said I'd give her lots of time and if I kiss her now, the last thing I'll be thinking about is giving her more time.

"Show me the rest of the house, you big softie," she says in that teasing tone. I like it when she teases me. I like the way it makes her eyes sparkle.

She pauses in the living room when she sees the big Christmas tree. Most of the trees grown here at the ranch are Fraser Firs. It's the tree that ninety percent of Christmas tree farmers grow in the state.

But the one in my living room is a Carolina Sapphire. Once I learned they were Cassie's favorite, I made sure we started growing them. They're different than our usual product. The needles look more blue than green, and the trees smell of minty citrus.

Micah wasn't too sure about investing in them at first but they're becoming in demand across the

South. Not that I can say it was a business decision I made with my head. I just wanted things around the ranch that gave my girl a reason to smile.

"It's incredible," she whispers and reaches out to touch the branches.

"I'm still working on growing them," I explain. It takes years to grow Christmas trees. People think you just plop one down in the ground and five minutes later, you've got a tree. No, when you're planting Christmas trees, you're playing the long game. It could be years before they're the right size to harvest. Granted, this particular type grows rapidly but I'm still not ready to bring them to market until I know we've got everything optimized for them. "We're hoping to start selling them in the next three years."

I gesture toward the boxes of decorations in the floor by my couch. That was something else I liberated from my parents' place. They have hundreds of decorations, more than they can ever use each year. But they're constantly sharing them with friends and family, so I took a few. I looked for things that would make Cassie happy. "Could use some help decorating it."

She tugs off her coat and tosses it to the couch. "Let's start with the lights."

I bought about a million of them all in different colors. I have big bulbs and little ones. I have white lights and colored lights. I have ones that blink and can be controlled with your cellphone.

We spend the next hour, decorating the tree as her favorite Christmas movie plays in the background. It's some love story that always makes her misty-eyed. But I don't care what she plays as long as we're together.

"What was your favorite Christmas?" I ask her after we finish hanging the final strand of lights. She went with the ones that blink all different colors, saying they look best with this type of tree.

She shakes her head. "You go first."

I don't even have to think about it. There's one celebration that stands out among all of them for me. It's the one that changed my life, the one where I gave away my heart. "The Christmas you came to live with us."

She looks up at me, tears springing to her eyes. "Really?"

"I fell in love that year." I've never been the same since.

All those years and I didn't understand why my dad always said that falling in love changes how you see everything. Then I fell in love with Cassie and suddenly, I did understand. Because you stop being the most important person in your world.

Suddenly, that space belongs to the person you care about. Their dreams, hopes, and joy become central to your own happiness, and you'd do anything for them. The way I'd do anything just to make Cassie happy.

"It was my favorite Christmas too," she admits.

Then I'm kissing her again. My hands are everywhere, trying to feel every inch of her curvy body, the way I've always longed to. My fingers tangle in her hair before skimming down her and gripping her round ass. She swings her legs around my waist, and I carry her to the couch. The entire time, she's pressing kisses to my face and neck, anywhere she can get those pouty lips.

I sit with her in my lap and instantly reach for the buttons on her shirt. Fuck, it's been killing me since she walked in the house. I've been wondering what color her bra is and what kind she likes to wear. Is it those plain serviceable ones? Something with satin or lace? I don't really care, just as long as my curiosity can finally be satisfied.

She puts her hands over mine and instantly, I still. I want her more than I want my next breath, but her needs come first always.

"West..." She says my name so softly and so tentatively. "I...I'm not ready for everything yet."

"And by everything?" I ask. I'm pretty sure I know where she's heading with this discussion, but I don't want to get this wrong. We've spent years dancing around each other, telling half-truths. I want those days to be over and done. We're honest with each other now.

"Sex," she finally murmurs. Only she's not looking at me. She's staring at the buttons on my shirt.

"Are you...?" I don't even know how to finish the sentence. All this time I've saved myself for her, but I never imagined she'd be doing the same thing. Never thought I'd get to be her first and only.

She nods. "Nobody ever made me ache like you do."

Primal satisfaction goes through me at her words. I'm the only one who can get her worked up and horny. The only one who can delight her body like this. I take a deep breath and press my forehead against hers. "We don't have to do everything. But I want to make you feel good tonight."

"Like on the sleigh?" There's a slight tremor to her voice that I find adorable. Everything about this woman gets me going.

"But better this time." My cock is leaking just remembering how tightly her channel clenched around my finger.

"I don't think it gets better," she says.

"Let's find out." This time when I reach for her buttons, she lets me. She lets me unbutton her shirt until I'm glimpsing her pink bra with the little white bow in the center. Her breasts swell over the cups, revealing full tits that I can't wait to get my mouth all over.

Her cheeks are pink and she's still not looking at me.

I put my finger under her chin, raising it. "Don't look away like this is something to be embarrassed about. There's nothing wrong about what's happening between us."

She licks her lip that's still swollen from where I was kissing her. "We're different, West."

I can't help grinning. She's all soft curves and I'm hard ridges. She's sunshine and joy while I'm the driving rain and grouchiness. It's why we fit together so perfectly. "That's the point."

"No, I mean. You've got like this." She gestures up and down my chest. "And I'm...fluffy."

I finally understand what she's saying. She's self-conscious and the realization floors me. I squeeze her ass, hoping my fingerprints are on it tomorrow morning. "If you only knew how often I've worked my cock to the sight of these curves. In my mind, I've taken you in every possible position. I've had you on your knees, on your back, on your stomach. And every single time, it was the thought of this curvy body that had me coming in my hand and shouting your name."

Her blush darkens but she gives me a small grin. "You touched yourself to thoughts of me?"

"Damn straight I did," I answer. "For ten years all I've thought about is how good it would feel to fuck my best friend's little sister. How pretty your tits would be, how noisy you'd be, how tight your cunt would feel around my cock."

She gasps at my filthy speech. Instead of slapping me for it, she reaches for the clasp in the back and shrugs out of the bra. Just like that, I'm staring at perfection. Her pale pink tits put all of my fantasies to shame. She's even better than every dirty dream I've had.

I lean forward and suck one nipple into my mouth, swirling my tongue around the tight bud. She arches into me and tugs on my hair, but I don't stop. I can't stop. I've been obsessed with this woman for ten years and now I have to know exactly what gets her off.

After a long minute, I move to the other breast to give it the same tender attention. There's something so damn satisfying about having your woman's tits in front of your face, about knowing you're giving her an experience she's never gotten with anyone else.

She's squirming on my lap and begging for mercy by the time I finally release her. I love the sight of her nipples shining from my mouth. "Touch me again," she pleads.

"I want to taste you this time," I tell her. I got a tiny taste earlier in the sleigh, but it wasn't enough. I don't think it'll ever be enough with this woman. I need my lips and fingers and cock on her all the time. My reason for existence has suddenly become clear and it's to please this beautiful woman writhing on my thighs.

She's too far gone to feel self-conscious because she gives a jerky nod and lets me help her out of her skirt.

I lay her back on the couch and pull down her panties slowly, watching her reaction. But she doesn't look embarrassed or nervous like she did earlier. No, now she looks enraptured, like she can't wait to see what I do next.

She's got a nice full bush and for some crazy reason, that excites me. I love knowing that nothing gets to touch her down here. Not even a razor.

Slowly, I spread her pussy lips and take a moment to savor the view of all the glistening pink perfection. It's for me. All that beautiful flesh belongs to me. She's mine to protect. Mine to love. Mine to please.

Ducking my head, I inhale her scent before I run my tongue through her delicate folds. Her flavor explodes on my tongue, and I know I could die a happy man now. Because I've tasted the sweetest dessert in the world and it's my woman's pussy.

"You're addictive," I growl against her swollen flesh, feeling her juices coat my face and beard. It's the sexiest feeling in the world, knowing that she's making a mess on my face.

I lap at Cassie until she's thrashing beneath me. She's muttering incoherently and begging me not to stop. But I still don't show her any mercy. I just put my hands around her hips to anchor her to the spot. She's not getting away from me. Not now when we've just started to find our way together.

Just when she's a begging mess, I suck her clit

into my mouth. She comes with a cry of ecstasy so loud that I'm sure it's going to ring in my ears for the rest of my life. Savage satisfaction fills me at the noise. I did that. I drove my woman over the edge.

She grins up at me lazily as she floats back down to earth. "I was wrong. It does get better."

5
CASSIE

West's face is covered in my juices and his hair is messy from where I kept running my fingers through it. But that look on his face is everything. He's staring down at me with so much emotion in his eyes that it makes me wonder how we both managed to hide our feelings from each other for so long.

I let out a soft giggle, still high from the two orgasms he ate me through. "I was wrong. It does get better."

He winks at me. "Got more where that came from, sweetheart."

That's twice now that he's touched me, given me orgasms and hasn't once asked for me to return the favor. I sit up carefully, no longer overcome by the urge to hide my body from his knowing gaze. He's seen everything I have, and he likes it. When he talked about spending ten years fisting his cock to fantasies of me, I thought I was going to burst into flames. It's the sexiest thing I've ever heard.

But now I want to give him the same pleasure he gives me. I reach for the waistband of his jeans. I don't know how to do any of this because no other guys have ever existed in my mind. I've never wanted to touch anyone else, feel anyone else in my hand. It's different with West though.

To my surprise, West gently removes my hands from his waistband. He presses kisses to my knuckles. "We're not doing that tonight."

I swallow hard, trying not to feel embarrassed. "Is it because I don't know what I'm doing?"

He smiles against my hands and his wet beard is soft and silky. "If my cock comes out to play, what little of my self-control is left will snap. You'll be under me and screaming my name in less than two minutes. But you aren't ready for that yet."

"Oh," my breath comes out as a shudder. How is it that I've spent so long around this man, and this is the first time we've done these things? If only we'd gotten together ten years ago, we could have a decade of experience together. "But aren't you kind of miserable?"

He pulls me into his lap, not caring that I'm naked or dripping onto his pants. He covers me in a blanket before he wraps his arms around me. "I've spent a decade waiting for you, a few more months isn't going to kill me. When we have our first time together, I want you to know you're mine. There won't be any regrets between us."

I smile against his chest. I can't imagine that I'd ever regret being with West but I'm glad that he understands I need time. I have to figure this out because I want it all. I want a life with this grumpy cowboy beside me. I want to stay at the ranch and continue to make toys. Maybe even have kids of our own someday.

The piercing noise of the smoke alarm startles us from our cocoon of warmth. He quickly sets me down and goes to stop the alarm. While he does that, I search the living room for my clothes and dress myself again.

By the time I'm decent, he's already pulled the burned dish from the oven. He scowls down at the offending casserole as well as what might have been some type of poultry but now is too blackened to be recognizable.

"It's OK. I'd have rather had the dessert you gave me on the couch," I say trying to reassure him. It really isn't a big deal. Just that he took the time to cook one of my favorite dishes for me means a lot.

He grins up at me. "I have frozen meals."

So that's how we end up eating frozen meals from the microwave on our first date. I don't even care that the turkey is slimy, and the mashed potatoes still have frozen bits in them. Because I'm getting to spend time with West.

"What are you smiling about?" He asks as he tries to stab into his brownie. The treat is still frozen despite him microwaving it repeatedly. I don't think it's ever going to thaw.

I can't stop grinning tonight. My cheeks hurt from how happy I feel. "Well, it's just, we're dating now, and I got to thinking that makes you my boyfriend. My first boyfriend."

"And it makes you my girlfriend," he answers, taking his hand in mine.

I push away the plastic tray, no longer interested in our dinner. He's rubbing his thumb along the back of my hand in a comforting gesture.

I let out a little sigh, wondering what his parents would think if they heard him call me his girlfriend. I overheard them years ago, warning him away from me. They told him he could never date me. If they made me leave, would he follow? Would he be willing to give up all of this?

The questions make me worry about the future. A million what-ifs swirl through my brain as my stomach tightens. "Do you like working the family ranch now?"

In his senior year, he blew out his knee during football practice. It was right before the championship game. His team lost state and all of his college scholarship offers were rescinded. He was angry for a long time after that.

"I couldn't imagine doing anything else now," he says, oblivious to the real question I'm asking him. He's so normal, always so calm. Meanwhile, one thought sends me into a tailspin and it's all I can focus on.

He's never leaving. I realize that with a start. Even if he wanted to leave, his parents are sick, and he's been stepping up to help them out more. That's not likely to change in the next few years. As they continue to age, they're going to need him in other ways too.

I can't think on these things right now or I'll start doing that thing where it gets really hard to breathe.

I push back from the table and stand. "Let's finish the Christmas tree."

We work together in silence for several long moments before West asks, "What do you want from Santa this year?"

To feel like I belong. To not have to worry about being asked to leave. To see your smile every day for the rest of my life. "There's nothing I want."

"There's nothing you want?" He deadpans in a tone that clearly indicates he doesn't believe me.

"I have everything I could possibly want right here," I tease before standing on my tip toes to press a chaste kiss to his lips. His beard tickles my face and I love the sensation, especially when I remember that it was wet from my essence just an hour ago.

He frowns at me. "What was your life like before the Kringle Ranch?"

I twine a small red bow around the Christmas tree. Mom loves to add bows of all colors to her trees. She says it's because the holidays are a gift, and we should never take them for granted.

"I don't know. I don't remember much until I was about six. That's when Micah and I got taken from our mom." There are other things before that. I have more memories, but I don't ever reach for them. I know that my brother is scarred and never talks about before. He's told me that our past doesn't matter. Given the sad look on his face when he says it, I think it's probably a good thing I don't remember.

"And the homes after that?" He sorts through the ornaments, putting the snowflakes and icicles in separate piles.

"Some of the families were nice," I admit. OK, so most of them were nice to Micah. He's easy to love. He always does what other people want and never asks for anything for himself. He's not needy or anxious. He works hard and he always excels at whatever he tries. "Everybody loved Micah."

"But they didn't love you?" He looks up from his work, his beautiful brown gaze holding me hostage.

"Not everyone is easy to love." It hurts to admit those words out loud. It hurts to tell West who I really like the painful truth. But he'll figure it out if he's with me long enough. Maybe that's why his parents warned him against pursuing me.

"Cassie—" I can't pick out the note in his voice. I'm not sure if it's a reprimand or pity or shock. But it doesn't matter. I can't change who I am. I can hide it for a little while, but my true self always comes back to the surface.

"I think your tree looks really good." I step back

and gesture toward it. "Maybe you should put a few more ornaments on the bare spots. But you have a great frame and I need to go now. They'll be wondering where I am."

He blows out a breath. I can see there's more he wants to say. It's written on his face but finally he nods. "Let me grab my coat."

"You don't have to. It's not far."

"My girlfriend doesn't walk home alone in the dark," he growls.

I manage a smile at his bossy tone. I should have known he wouldn't let me. West has always been fiercely protective over me.

When we're outside, he holds my hand. Maybe I should say something about it. After all, anyone passing upon us would be able to tell we're holding hands. But I like the feeling of his big fingers wrapped around mine too much.

I like the way it feels to have his steady presence beside me as we trudge down the familiar path that has footprints in it already. Probably from Micah and Ledger. They've been visiting Mom and Dad every day since he came home from the hospital.

We thought he was having a heart attack, but we were fortunate. It was a close call and the doctor warned him that one is around the corner if he doesn't change his lifestyle.

As we approach the house, the porchlight is on and glowing. It always is because Dad will wait up for me. He's an early to bed and early to rise type. Except when we were teenagers. Then he'd stay up late and pretend to build a model boat. He's been building the same one since I was in high school.

West squeezes my fingers as we approach the front porch. He pauses before we get to the light and turns to me. He brushes a gentle kiss to my forehead. "For the record, you are incredibly easy to love."

Then he's gone, fading back into the shadows of the night. I stand there and stare into the darkness until I can't see him anymore. I should probably go inside but I'm rooted to the spot for the longest time. I think I'm falling in love with West Kringle.

6
WEST

"This had better be a damn good emergency," I tell Micah as I pound on his front door. He called me a few minutes ago and woke me from a dream about Cassie. She was naked and in the shower with me. I'd just pulled her against me when my phone went off.

This is probably what my mom would call a blessing in disguise. It gives me a chance to come clean to my best friend, to tell him that I'm dating his sister. He deserves to hear it from me, man-to-man. We'll deal with his emergency then I'll tell him that I'm in love with his sister and keeping her forever.

He opens the door, looking even more disgruntled than I feel. He's holding a sleeping baby in his arms. "This is what I called you for."

"No, thanks. I don't want it," I answer, only half teasing him. There are dark circles under his eyes. He's taken over so much since Dad had the health scare. He's always worked the hardest here. Sometimes, it's like he has to prove he's earned his place. After what Cassie said last night about not being lovable, it makes me wonder what wounds the system left on him.

"She got left on my doorstep," he explains. "Tiny wisp of a thing with only a blanket and a bag of formula. Look at her. Too damn chilly for that."

I've never seen Micah date a woman. He's always been too interested in this farm, same as me and Ledger. But Micah is the one that travels. Dad sends him when we need a friendly face for our biggest clients. Guess he must have had some fun on one of those trips. "Is she yours?"

He murmurs almost to himself, "She is now."

I scratch at my beard. "How old is she? Where's her mama? What's her name?"

He stares at her, a frown creasing his forehead. "I don't know her age. Had to check the damn diaper to even figure out she's my daughter. She doesn't have a name. Least not that I've been able to find." He gestures me deeper into his house.

I follow him into the warmth, noticing the way he cradles her so carefully. He's holding her just like you're supposed to hold a baby. I guess that's an advantage of working around the Christmas tree farm. We're constantly being handed kids to take pictures with.

He walks to the living room where there's a car seat on the coffee table. A fire crackles as Sinatra croons out another love song. In the corner, his Christmas tree adds a soft glow to everything. It looks like a scene from a Christmas card, except for the baby whose name we don't know.

"That's all I have on her," his voice carries a broken note.

My heart hurts for him. He got drunk one night a few years back and talked about how hard it is to be nine years old and handed a garbage bag to shove all your stuff into. That's if the social worker is kind enough and patient enough to wait for you in the first place. Sometimes, you leave with only the clothes on your back and that happens to hundreds of kids across the country every single day. Uprooted from their latest placement with nothing to soothe or comfort them.

I examine the basket and little bag. It has two bottles with formula and a note. It's short and sweet. *She's yours. Take good care of her, Micah.*

"Fuck," I breathe out.

He scowls at me and gestures toward the baby. "Don't cuss in front of my daughter."

Pretty sure his daughter is sleeping too deeply to hear, much less care about the language I'm using.

"Cash is on his way to check her out," he says. Cash Taylor is the local doctor. He's married with kids of his own and a ranch to run. Yet he never turns away a patient, no matter how rural their location or how poor their family. He lives and breathes for the people of this town and we're lucky to have him.

"You should have taken him to her. It would have been faster," I answer, peering at the bundle again. Her cheeks are a nice rosy pink, and her breaths are even.

"I don't think she was out there for long," he says. "I heard a racket on the porch and got out of bed to investigate."

"She's awfully tiny," I say as I imagine Cassie holding one of ours. Looks like I won't be telling Micah I'm dating his sister today. He's got enough on his plate. But I'll make sure to tell him soon. I don't want him finding out any other way.

"She's got a warrior's spirit though," he answers with a soft smile at her. He's clearly already bonding with her.

Headlights sweep in through the front window, alerting us to the fact that Cash has arrived for the baby's checkup. "Should I stay?"

He shakes his head. "I won't be in today, so it'll be all hands on deck."

"Don't you worry about that," I reassure him. "You just look after the little one. Everything else will come together."

I'm not entirely sure about that last part. Micah handles a lot of management tasks for Dad. He's the smart one. Give him a dollar and next thing you know, he has a hundred. It's the same concept with the farm. It was doing well for decades. But under Micah's guidance, our profits consistently double.

I nod to the little one. "And congratulations."

He manages a smile that might be more of a grimace. "Thanks."

My day is a blur of chaos without Micah to smooth everything over. I didn't tell Mom and Dad what was going on. I just told them Micah wasn't feeling well and left it at that. They'll figure out what's happening pretty soon.

In the meantime, I've been working like hell to get my usual work done in addition to fielding a million questions from the employees. I've come to the conclusion that Micah does not get paid enough for the shit he deals with.

The only bright spot is the text messages that Cassie and I exchange. They have me smiling at my phone all day long.

"What's your deal?" Ledger asks while he wolfs down a sandwich in the back office with me. "You been smiling like a fool all damn day."

Like Micah and Cassie, Ledger was adopted by my folks when he was a teenager. He was a firecracker in high school, always doing something crazy and wild. My best memories from back then involve him pulling me and Micah into some outrageous stunt.

I open a bag of chips. Does everyone around here think I'm the big green guy? "What's wrong with being happy?"

"It's creepy when you're smiling." Ledger washes

down a bite of his food with a long sip of water. "Wait...did you get laid last night?"

I'm not the type of man that would kiss and tell. It's nobody's business what two consenting adults do but more than that, this is Cassie. I'll always be overprotective when it comes to her, so I settle for a warning grunt.

"Peyton will be there tonight," he tells me to change the subject. Peyton is Ledger's best friend, a girl he's been in love with since they were in high school together. I don't know how she feels about him though. The bartender of Liquid Courage plays everything close to the vest.

"Are you going to tell her how you feel?" It's what I ask him every Christmas. He swears he'll tell her when the time is right. But we both know the moment he tells her how he feels, she's going to bolt like a deer that caught scent of a predator.

"Soon." It's what he always says.

"You know she was supposed to help Cassie finish the set up with Santa's workshop today, but she called out because of a migraine." He finishes off the rest of his sandwich and shakes his head. "Michael volunteered to help out though. They're all alone over there. Putting up Christmas lights, probably listening to some golden oldies. I'm sure it's not cozy and romantic at all."

I toss my half-eaten food on the desk then shoot to my feet so fast my desk chair rolls back and bangs into the wall. My woman does not spend time alone around other men. Definitely not men that look at her like she's a tasty treat. She's *my* treat. She's only for my hands and eyes and tongue.

He laughs then and I realize I tipped my entire damn hand. He knows who I'm dating.

"You're a bastard."

"Sounds about right," he mutters.

I ignore his glee as I shove my keys and wallet in my pocket. "Try not to let this place fall down around your ears while I'm gone."

He gives me a sarcastic salute that I'm too busy to even care about. There's only one thing on my mind right now and that's getting back to my girl.

The drive to the community center doesn't take long and before I know it, I'm marching inside. My anger grows with every step. He's not taking her from me. No one is. She's my girl and I'll never let her go.

I step inside the community center and see her standing in the middle of the decorations as she surveys her work. I stomp up to her. I spin her around and pull her into my arms. Then I lower my head and kiss her until we're both gasping for air.

"I don't share," I growl when I finally pull away long enough to let us both breathe. "Not with Michael. Not with anybody."

She giggles then, a small tinkling sound. "That's good to know. But I'm here alone."

The fight drains out of me as I realize I've been had. Damn Ledger and his love for practical jokes. Though I can't say I really hate this one since it led me back to my girl.

Her eyes are sparkling as she says, "But since you're here, I could use help with a few things, boyfriend."

7
CASSIE

My back is aching, and my feet hurt but it's finally done. The community center has been transformed into Santa's workshop, just like it always is every year. I added a few fun touches this time.

I snap a couple of pictures that hint at what I've done and send them to Mom and Dad. Hopefully, they'll love these additions. They promised they'd drive into town and stay for a few minutes of the event. I think Dad would still be dressed up as Santa Claus if Mom didn't put her foot down and demand that he relax this year.

One of the doors to the center open and I hear someone stomping across the worn linoleum. But I don't even have to turn. I know from the sound of the footsteps that West is here.

I wait, my body filled with wild anticipation. Then he grabs me, spins me around, and kisses me breathless.

He makes an animalistic noise deep in his throat when he finally releases me long enough to let me breathe. "I don't share. Not with Michael. Not with anybody."

I didn't think this man could get any sexier but seeing this possessive side to him is making my panties damp all over again. I squeeze my thighs together, trying to ignore the building tension. "That's good to know. But I'm here alone."

His entire stance relaxes and the tension bleeds from his muscles. He was coming in here prepared for a fight that would never happen. Because I know who I belong to. I know I'm his and I'd never even look in the direction of another man.

"But since you're here, I could use help with a few things, boyfriend."

He quirks an eyebrow and his voice is deep when he asks, "What things?"

We manage to get about halfway through the remaining items on my to do list before he gives into temptation. When we're in one of the back rooms where I've stashed extra toys for the kids, he pins me against the wall with his body in one fluid motion.

He presses his lips against my neck before nipping at the sensitive skin. "You've been teasing me today."

"Yes," I answer, unable to lie to him. His manhood is almost where I need it. I try to wiggle my hips to get some friction, but he pushes more weight against me. He's pinned me in place and grabbed my wrists. He's holding them over my head with just one of his hands. The way he's so big and so powerful makes me feel tiny and defenseless, like he owns me. But I love that idea, the thought that I could be West's property to do with as he pleases.

He's teasing me too. He's letting his fingertips trace the inside of my thigh through my tights. Every time he gets close to my pussy, he starts over again. He's leaving me aching and eager with every gentle motion.

"Why, little girl?" His gaze searches my face, wondering about this game we're playing. He wants to know everything about me and why I do the things I do. He wants to understand what I'm asking for and he'll give it to me. It's written in his expression.

"Because I need you." I'm nearly ready to sob at this point. I need his lips on me and his fingers touching me. I need this man to give me everything. "Tonight. After the celebration, I want *everything*."

He stops tracing my thigh, but he doesn't let go of me. I'm still pinned between the wall and his hard body, completely at his mercy. He brushes a strand of hair from my face. "I've waited for you since I was eighteen. I'll wait another decade if you just say the word."

"Wait, does that mean you haven't slept with any woman since you met me?" The idea pleases me more than it should. I never asked if he was seeing anyone. I purposely tried to ignore it any time the subject of girls came up around my brothers. I couldn't stand the idea of knowing that some other girl was getting his kisses and touches.

He chuckles and the warm affection in his gaze wraps around me like a fuzzy blanket on a cold, winter night. "I never slept with anyone before you either."

I can't help grinning. No one has ever been with West. No woman has ever known him the way I'll get to know him. "So, we'll be each other's firsts?"

"First and last," he promises me.

"Kiss me again," I plead. The ache in my body is now an inferno and I need this big man all over me. I'm pretty sure my panties melted away at some point between our conversation and now there's only molten lava between my legs.

He sweeps his tongue into my mouth, kissing me desperately and passionately. He kisses me until I'm dizzy from a lack of oxygen and drugged on his taste. I'm just about to beg him to take me right here in the community center when the door opens.

We spring apart like we're a couple of horny teenagers caught making out in the park after-hours. I adjust my rumpled clothes and try to finger-comb my hair. But it's no use, our visitor will be able to tell exactly what was happening in here. Especially because West has a very prominent bulge in the front of his pants. No amount of adjusting will hide that monster.

"Hey, baby, where are you?" Mom calls out.

My stomach knots. *She'll figure this out.*

Before I can say anything, Mom is coming into the room. Her big luggage-size purse is slung over her shoulder and her arms are loaded down with more of her quilts. She works all year to make them only to give them away. It's the kind of selfless person she is. She pauses when she takes in West's appearance and mine. There's a knowing glint in her eye.

West doesn't flinch or shrink down. He eyes his mom with calm reassurance. "I'm not ashamed of this."

She sets her quilts down on a stack of boxes. "Let me talk to Cassie alone."

I gulp in air, my heart slowing down. Is it still beating? Is this what it feels like when your heart breaks? Maybe it's not a shattering. Maybe it just slowly stutters to a stop, and you can't feel it anymore.

To my surprise, West looks to me. I've never known him to defy his mom. He respects her too much to challenge her, even when he believes she's wrong. But he's waiting for my approval. Just like that, I realize I'm the woman he'll look to now, the one he listens to first. I wonder if she'll hate me for that.

I give him the slightest nod.

He leans forward to brush a kiss across my forehead. "I'll finish up those changes we talked about."

He moves to leave the room but pauses before he does. He whispers something to his mom and her face lights up. He's always known how to make her smile.

Then he leaves the room, closing the door behind himself. The doorknob clicks into place and we're alone.

My mom focuses her attention on me. She studies me, her curls bouncing when she tips her head. Her hair is red now, no streaks of gray. She must have made it to the salon today.

I wait for her to say something first but we just end up staring at each other. She's looking at me as if she's never seen me until this moment and it guts me. I live in her house. I call her mom. I make pecan pies with her every Saturday night. "Do I have to leave now?"

She frowns, the lines on her face becoming more prominent. They weren't always there. But after Dad, everything changed. Now they've both aged a century in just a few weeks. "You mean, move out of the house?"

My throat is clogged and it's hard to get out the words. "Do I have to leave the ranch?"

"Why would you do that?"

She's going to make me say it. Make me face the truth. "Because I like West. I know you don't want me to be with him. You warned him away from me years ago when I first came to live with all of you. And I understand. I'm not your real daughter. I'm not anybody's daughter."

I don't belong to anyone. I was starting to think maybe I belonged to West, that we would be together. But I can't ask him to leave his parents. They need him.

"You stop that right now." Mom straightens her spine, raising herself to her full five feet of height. She has the same fierce expression she wore when the Sunday school teacher tried to shame me for wearing a dress that would "lead boys to sin". She put Mr. Chambers in his place right then and there. Never again was I shamed for what I wore to church. Or anywhere.

Her voice shakes with emotion when she says, "You are my daughter. You were my daughter long before the ink was dry on that adoption paperwork. It took us time to find each other, but you have always been mine."

Her words touch some aching, broken place in my heart and it begins to stitch itself back together again. My eyes fill with tears, and I press a hand against my mouth.

"As for West, I warned him away. That's true. It never had to do with being ashamed of you. Honey, how old were you when you came to live with us?"

"Fifteen," I answer, sniffing.

"You were seen as a child in the eyes of the law," she says. "And he was eighteen, a legal adult. Even if you'd been of age, you were just coming out of the foster system. You were still having nightmares and crying yourself to sleep. You weren't in a place where it would have been healthy. Not for either of you."

Her words make me see the situation differently. She wasn't trying to protect West from some girl who was beneath him. She was trying to protect both of our hearts. I accept the tissue she passes me and dab at my eyes. "And what do you think now?"

"Now, I think my son has chosen well." She gives me a soft smile, her own eyes filled with tears. "When he walked out of here, he warned me to be gentle. He called you his heartbeat. I always hoped you two would find your way to each other."

I rush forward and wrap my arms around this woman who has been my mentor and my friend and my mom. She's never hesitated to defend me from others or step into my messes or listen as I had a good cry. "Thank you."

"And I forgive you," she says as she pats my back.

"For what?" I sniff, mystified as to what I said earlier that could have hurt her feelings.

She chuckles. "For wrecking the Mustang all those years ago."

I pull away to search her face. But there's no anger in her expression, only amusement. "You knew?"

"Honey, a mother always knows," she answers with a wink.

8
CASSIE

Why won't these people all just go home? Why do they insist on putting their sticky kids on Santa's lap and taking a dozen photos with him? Alright, maybe I'm feeling a little grumpy because I want to knock the kids out of the way and sit on Santa's lap instead. Only instead of telling him what I want for Christmas, I'll tell him about my dirtiest fantasies.

It doesn't help that West keeps glancing at me across the room. The look in his eyes is pure fire. He's not bothering to hide his desire and every glance feels like a caress.

My phone dings and it's a message from Micah. He's the only one left that doesn't know. Mom told Dad when he arrived. But he didn't seem to care. He just gave me a big hug and told me I'd always be his girl. Ledger even knows if the smirk he was sending West tells me anything.

Sorry I couldn't make it. Talk tomorrow.

West said he was sick. He had that funny hitch in his voice, but he wouldn't tell me anything else. He said that Micah wasn't as bad off as I was thinking and that I'd have to get the full story from him.

I send a message back. *Try to get some extra sleep.*

His little dots appear to show he's typing. They disappear and reappear before another message comes through. *You too.*

I snort. That's not likely if everything goes the way I'm hoping. But I can't tell him that. Instead, I settle for telling Micah I love him and closing out of the messages. Tomorrow, we'll talk, and I'll get the chance to clear the air.

For now, the night belongs to me and my grumpy cowboy.

"Are we done here?" West asks. He's changed out of his Santa costume and into his usual jeans and plaid button up. All of the families have gone home. We're the last two people left in the community center since it's my job to lock up tonight.

"Almost finished," I answer, scooping up the last of the paper plates. I turn toward the kitchenette. Tonight was a smashing success. We gave out twice as many toys this year and helped a record fifty-five needy families. But the best part was seeing the pride on Mom and Dad's faces as we pulled everything off. I have a feeling this might just become an annual tradition for me and West.

He slings an arm around my waist, stopping me. His lips are so close to my ear and his breath is so hot. "Are you running from me?"

"Would that put me on the naughty list?" I mean to ask the question to distract him, so I can slip away and finish straightening up the room. But the question comes out flirty and suggestive in a way I didn't mean.

West's eyes darken. "Do you want to be on that list?"

I chew my bottom lip, loving the way his gaze tracks the simple motion. "It depends on what happens to naughty girls."

He chuckles then, the sound rough and dangerous. "You'll have to come back to my place to find out."

"I packed a bag," I admit, my cheeks growing warm. I left halfway through the event when everyone else was distracted to pack an overnight bag. Mom and Dad know where I'll be tonight, so they won't be up late worrying.

"I like the way you think." He presses a kiss to my nose and holds out his hand. "Come on. Let's get out of here."

The entire ride back to West's place, he holds my hand. We're silent as he navigates his aging truck through the slick, snow-covered roads. But it's not an awkward silence. It's a comforting one. We know each other so well that we don't have to talk when we're together.

"You need lights on the front porch," I finally tell him when he pulls into his driveway. There's nothing sadder than coming home to a dark house. I always hated that when I was a foster kid. "You need something warm and welcoming."

He squints up at the dark house, as if seeing it for the first time. "Then you should pick something out and I'll install it."

"It's your house. You need to do stuff that you like. But maybe a garden out front. Ooh, and a little wishing well."

"It's not my house anymore. It's *our* house," he answers.

My heart warms at the words. This thing

between us is still so new that I haven't spent a lot of time thinking about our future together. But now that we can be out in the open, all of the possibilities are right there. "You want me to move in here with you?"

"I want everything with you, Cassie. I want the house and the wedding and the kids and your crazy hissing cat."

I chuckle. "Snowball likes you."

"Well, she has good taste." He takes my hand and tugs me from the warmth of his truck. "Come on. You've been on your feet all night, taking care of everyone else. Let me take care of you now."

He guides me to his bathroom where he has an oversized tub and walk-in shower. Pretty sure Micah was the one who told him to do this. He probably told him it would drive the value of the property up.

He's always looking toward the future, always trying to take care of everyone. One day, I hope he finds a woman who takes care of him.

West starts the water and adds bubble bath with a lavender scent. I never imagined my grumpy cowboy would have a supply of bubble bath. Or that he could simply look at me and I'd feel myself melt.

While he busies himself gathering towels, I

gather my hair into a hot pink scrunchie and peel my clothes from my body. By the time he's back, I'm standing naked in the warm bathroom as the floral scent fills the air.

"Fuck." He drops the towels and grabs the center of his jeans. "That's a hell of a sight to walk in on."

I shake my head at him even as I light up under his praise. There's something special about knowing the man I'm with finds me irresistibly sexy. "You're still wearing too many clothes for a bath, Mr. Kringle."

He glances between me and the filling tub. "I said you were going to take a bath."

I fake a pout. "You won't join me?"

"Hell yeah, I will." He's out of his own clothes before he's even finished talking and for the first time, I'm seeing my brother's best friend naked. The sight makes my mouth go dry. All of that beautiful golden skin exposed to me and those tattoos that start on his forearms trace all the way up to his broad shoulders.

His pecs are dotted with dark hair that I can't wait to run my fingers through. His stomach is flat but there's no six-pack here and I love that. My man is at a healthy size and glancing down further, that's not the only thing that's a healthy size. My gaze widens when I see his cock with his big hand wrapped around it.

I gulp at the sheer size and his chuckle has me dragging my gaze back up to his face. "We'll figure it out."

I nod because I trust him. West always looks out for me. He's always doing what's best for me and sex won't be any different. He'll put me first. It's what he does.

He helps me into the tub but not before I displace a lot of water. He just laughs it off and settles into the tub beside me. I don't know if it's the warm water or the trust between us, but I love the feeling of being squished up against his big, naked body.

"Now, it's my turn to play." I reach for his silky shaft just beneath the water. I move my fingertips up and down it, studying his body.

He swears again under his breath. "Love the feeling of your fingers touching me."

"I love touching you." I squeeze him lightly, remembering the way he squeezed himself earlier. "Does that feel good?"

He groans and leans forward to take one of my nipples in his mouth. There's something about this that makes me feel so naughty. Having him suck my nipples while I jerk him off is making my pussy leak.

"Cassie…" He finally calls my name after we've spent long moments teasing each other. I slow my strokes. I'm learning that if I vary the pace, it keeps him from coming. "The first time I want to be inside of you."

I'm so achy and desperate that I make a whimper of agreement.

"Get on top of me," he commands in that deep, raspy tone of his.

"But I'll squish you." I'm pretty sure you can bend a guy wrong, can't you? I definitely don't want to bend him wrong.

"You won't squish me." He pants out another swear, and I glance up at his face. His eyes are wild, and his hair is mussed. "I don't have enough control to be gentle with you right now. If you're on top, you'll limit the angle and depth. I won't hurt you that way."

"Show me what to do," I tell him.

He guides me over his lap, and I'm squatting in the most awkward position ever. But I'm too nervous about hurting him to care about what he's looking at right now. "Alright, slide down nice and slow."

I hold my breath and align our bodies. I go down

slow, only getting a little in before I stop. It's too tight.

"Take your time," he says softly as he reaches to stroke my clit. His soft, teasing touch has the tension leaving my muscles and I manage to work in a little more.

When I feel his cock nudge my barrier, I take a deep breath and sit down. He impales me fully and I let out a soft hiss. The pain quickly gives way to pleasure and a feeling of fullness.

He runs his hands up and down my back. "How is it now?"

"Feels good. Really good. You?" I experiment with a small movement.

He groans. "Fucking perfect to me."

It takes a few tries but together, we slowly start to find a rhythm that has both of us gasping and panting. The entire time West is playing with my clit, sending me higher and higher.

"I'm there," I murmur.

"Then come for me," he says.

My nails dig into his thick shoulders as I finally surrender to the bliss he's giving me, losing myself in my body's sensations. It's only as I'm floating back down that I feel his release start. He comes with a guttural groan, sinking his teeth into my shoulder and marking me in a way no one else ever has.

We stay cuddled up together in the bathtub until the water grows cold. We're not saying a word, just holding each other as our heart rates return to normal. He breaks the silence to ask, "Did I hurt you?"

"That was perfect," I reassure him before I giggle. "I can't believe we just had sex for the first time."

There's a wicked gleam in his eye. "The first of many times."

"The first of many," I repeat back before I press a kiss to his lips.

9
CASSIE

"You're telling me you'd rather have X-ray vision than the ability to fly?" I demand of West as we sit at his kitchen table the next morning. Actually, he's sitting at his kitchen table. I'm on his lap because the moment I tried to sit down, he growled and pulled me over here.

Maybe it's because we've been pining for each other for ten years, but he hasn't stopped touching me since I walked in the door. Not that I'm complaining. He held me all through the night and was the first thing I saw when I opened my eyes today. "What advantage could X-ray vision possibly have over flying? You can get anywhere really fast."

He cuts another bite of his pancake and offers it to me. He's feeding me too. He's a total caveman who wants to do everything for me and I don't mind it. Actually, it feels kind of nice to have someone who just wants to take care of me. "Yeah, but with the vision, I can see you naked any time I want."

"Because I'm wearing so many clothes right now," I answer with an eyeroll. He's fully clothed and I'm sitting on his lap in just my panties and a see-through bra. In the floor by the kitchen island is my robe. I only got to wear it for three seconds before he was pulling it off of me and kissing his way down my skin. He ate me out twice before he made me chocolate chip pancakes with sprinkles. This man spoils me and the best part is I have a lifetime of us together to look forward to.

"Don't you get sassy with me, little girl," he says, giving my hip a firm squeeze. I love it when he calls me little girl. It's from his favorite Springsteen song and it always makes me smile.

Before I can make a smart retort, his front door swings open and Micah is barreling through the front door. He has a sleeping baby in his arms and my normally calm brother looks completely disheveled.

"Don't you know how to fuckin' knock?" West demands, doing his best to cover me by wrapping his arms around my body.

Micah takes in the two of us, me barely clothed and sitting on West's lap. His scowl deepens even more. "What the fu—hell are you doing with my naked sister?"

This has got to be the weirdest morning in the history of mornings. "Where did you get a baby? And turn around so I can put some clothes on."

He does as I instructed. "Someone left her on my doorstep. I don't know anything more than that. And how fuckin' long has this been going on?"

"Why the fuck are you here?" West grinds out.

I move to the kitchen island and grab my robe. But the material is sheer, so I'm still exposed. West shrugs out of his button-down and passes it to me, leaving him in a short-sleeved white t-shirt. It perfectly clings to his biceps, showcasing his strong muscles. "That doesn't answer anything. Is she yours? When did you—how do you have a daughter?"

"I don't know anything about her yet." Frustration and defeat bleed into Micah's tone. "All I know is she was there one morning and now I have to figure out how to help her."

"So, I have a niece?" In the middle of all the chaos, this thought registers and fills me with happiness. I always hoped that Micah would start a family one day. He's too serious, too in control. He needs a wife and kids to bring him joy and give him reasons to smile. Just like West does for me.

Micah ignores my question and talks to West instead, "Ledger called me this morning to tell me that you screwed up payroll. He's trying to calm the employees. But it's Christmas and they're counting on this money. I came over to sort out this mess."

"You can turn around now," I tell him when I'm covered again. Definitely going to make sure the doors are locked in the future. I didn't realize that the guys come and go between each other's houses. But it makes sense. They're all brothers and they're all single.

He glares at West. "That's my sister."

"And I'm in love with her," he says it with such absolute certainty.

"I don't give a fu...duck!" He finally substitutes when the sleeping bundle in his arms stirs.

I creep closer and peer at her. She has his nose. "Let me hold her."

He hesitates for a split second before he passes her to me, issuing instructions the entire time. "Support her head. Don't startle her. Talk softly. Cradle her close. She needs warmth."

I give him an amused smile. "She's pretty amazing."

Now that she's in my arms, Micah is free to turn all of his ire on West. I hope they're not going to come to blows over this. West wouldn't be the one to throw the first punch, I know that much. But if he thought he was defending my honor, he wouldn't hesitate to go to battle with my brother.

"I'm happy, Micah," I say quietly, hoping to defuse the tension.

"It's not about being happy," Micah snaps. "What happens when you break up? Where the fuck are we going to go then? I have a daughter to keep safe now. We can't go back to sleeping on park benches. Fuck, this is bad. You know what? I want both of you to forget this happened. We'll all three forget it and nothing bad will happen."

"I'm not breaking up with her," West answers. His tone is soft, but I can hear the steel in his voice. This man won't back down, not when it comes to me. "How many women have I been with? In all the time you've known me, who have I flirted with or taken home? No one. There's never been anyone because it's always been her. She's the only woman I've ever wanted."

In this moment, I finally understand just how

deeply our upbringing affected both of us. My heart aches for the kids we were, the ones who had to claw and struggle and fight just to survive. "We don't have to leave this time."

As I say the words, West crosses the kitchen. He slides an arm around my shoulders, pulling me close and offering me the comfort of his presence. Without a word, he's reassuring me that I'm right.

He shoves a hand through his hair, looking so much older than his twenty-eight years. "Of course, we have to leave. We always have to leave. People like us don't get warm homes and parents who care and enough to eat. Not if we're not good. We get kicked out."

"Fuck," West mutters under his breath. "Micah, listen to me. You're not a kid anymore."

The words seem to shake my brother and he's quiet for a long moment.

West continues, "No one can make you or Cassie leave. You're in the will. Did you know that? Mom and Dad state that you and Cassie and Ledger have equal shares. When they pass, we split the ranch. There's no division or difference made between the four of us. In their eyes, you're as much a Kringle as I am."

Micah rubs a spot on his chest. "I'm a Kringle?"

He was never legally adopted. There was no reason to fight the system for him once he was eighteen. I'm sure Mom and Dad figured it was just a formality since he was living with them and treated as their son. But I see it through Micah's eyes now. They adopted me and Ledger because we were still underage. West is their birth son. Micah is the only one who's never been officially called a Kringle.

"You're a Kringle," West repeats.

My brother looks between West and me. "You break her heart and I'll put you in the woodchipper out back. I'll do it slow too."

"I'll never give you a reason to do that." West crosses the kitchen to thump Micah on the back and give him a quick man hug. "You're a fuckin' Kringle. You own that shit right here and now."

Micah nods when he pulls away. "Now, let me help your fool ass fix payroll. I have to hire a nanny after this."

"In the meantime, maybe I could hold onto her for a few more minutes?" I ask, ruffling the sleeping girl's hair. It's so dark and thick. I wonder who her mama is and if she looks like her. There are so many questions I want to ask my brother but right now, all that matters is getting to spend time with my new niece.

Several hours later, West and Micah return. They seem as fine as ever, laughing and chatting about the next car they're going to restore. I guess they got out everything they needed to say earlier.

"She's had two bottles and slept except for a few minutes that she stared up at me," I tell Micah. "Maybe I could keep her just a little while longer?"

He scoops her up into his arms and smiles down at her. "Nah, you're behind on work and besides, I need to get some baby supplies and find my nanny."

"Where are you going to look?" I know sometimes you can get a nanny through an agency, but I think that takes time and Micah clearly needs someone to help him now.

"I don't know yet," he murmurs. "There's got to be someone in town who would like to spend their days holding her. If your boyfriend didn't fuck up payroll so badly, I'd retire and let him run the place."

"It'd be two days before I ran it into the ground and you know it," West answers. It's true. He is an amazing expert when it comes to every part of planting, growing, and packaging our trees. But he doesn't know anything about the business side of things. None of us do.

"I'll stop by for some auntie cuddles later." I pass him the diaper bag that's way too light for a baby. I'm pretty sure they come with a lot more accessories than he has. No wonder it's time for him to go into town for supplies.

"Yeah, she'd like that," he calls over his shoulder as he leaves the house.

Finally, I'm alone again with West. Even though there's plenty we should be doing, the only thing I really want is to snuggle with my man for a few minutes. I wrap my arms around him as I watch my brother leave. "She's adorable, isn't she?"

West presses a kiss to the top of my head. "I took you bare last night. That means we could have one of our own in nine months."

My heart skips a beat at the thought of having a little cowboy to chase around the house. "You wouldn't mind that?"

"I'd be over the moon," he reassures me. "I can't wait to raise a brood of our own the moment you're ready. But first, we need to talk."

"About what?"

He guides me to a kitchen chair and directs me to take a seat. Then he gets down in front of me on one knee. "You remember how I told you I need a

Christmas bride? Well, turns out I found her and I'm keeping her. Forever."

He pulls a jewelry box out of his pocket and opens it to reveal an oval-cut diamond that's huge. It's not just an engagement ring. It's a warning to any man that gets inside a twenty-foot radius of me. But that's OK. Because I like the warning.

I blink moisture from my eyes. "I want to be kept forever."

"I love you," he whispers before he slips the ring on my finger and presses a soft kiss to my lips. This grumpy cowboy is all mine and I'm his. Together, we're going to raise the next generation of Kringles right here on the family ranch.

EPILOGUE

WEST

"How much longer is this going to take?" I ask my mom as I pace up and down the aisle of the tiny chapel. It's been four weeks since I proposed to Cassie. Four weeks too long if you ask me.

I wanted to march her into the courthouse that very moment. My mom never would have forgiven me and besides, Cassie wanted a Christmas Eve wedding. Well, what my woman wants, she gets.

There's nothing I wouldn't do for her. If she told me she wanted me to stop the sun, I'd find a way to do that for her. She's everything to me which is why I'm so damn eager to tie the knot with her.

"It won't be long now," she reassures me. She leans over to pick some lint off Micah's suit coat. The chapel is tiny, only capable of holding a few people and we've filled it to capacity. Three generations of Kringles are here, all waiting in anticipation for the vows.

"Just tell her to put on some lipstick and get her cute ass out here," I insist.

Mom gasps like I just suggested that the green monster had it right all along. "Do you have any idea what a woman goes through to get ready for her wedding day? While you boys just roll out of bed and put on a suit—"

I know she's still talking, and I do my best to look contrite. But I can't focus anymore because the door opens, and I catch a peek of red lace.

My woman didn't want to go with a traditional white dress. She wanted a big red lacy thing. She could have told me she was planning to wear my old sweatshirt and a pair of her tight ass yoga pants, and I wouldn't have cared. I don't care about any of these details as long as I can call this beautiful woman mine before the end of the night.

She catches me staring and sends me a wink before Dad is ushering her to close the door.

The pastor, a local farmer who does weddings on the side, gestures for us to take our places. The old organ cranks out the wedding song but the tightness in my chest doesn't leave. It won't leave until he's announcing that we're wed. She's always been mine. Today is just a formality as far as I'm concerned. But I still want it to go perfectly for her.

The door swings open and just like that my beautiful bride is walking down the aisle. She's on my father's arm and her smile is so big that it could be considered blinding. Beside me, Micah's daughter makes a soft sniffing noise. He bounces her in his arm, quietly comforting her as Ledger stands nearby too. My brothers are my best men and it's only appropriate since they are the best men I know.

Mom stands on the bride's side with Chloe, the nanny that Micah hired. Peyton is also with them, and she keeps sneaking little peeks at Ledger. They're so in love with each other. Snowball purrs at my feet. She still hisses at everyone but me. It makes me laugh that she won't meow for anybody else. But despite all of my family around me, there's only one person I can focus on. My girl.

She takes my breath away with her beauty. She's glowing and we both know why. She peed on a stick last night. We were supposed to be apart, a night to make it all romantic. But she couldn't wait.

Cassie crashed the bachelor party to shove the stick in my face. I thought my heart was going to explode when I finally realized what it meant. I've never been happier or prouder in all my life than that moment. The moment I realized that I'd just become a father.

She's not feeling sick yet, which is a good thing because I plan to make the most of our honeymoon. I'm going to tire her little body out with endless orgasms. It's my favorite thing to do anyway. Every chance I get I have my lips, fingers, or cock giving her pleasure. It's what I was put on this earth to do—pleasure, provide, and protect this amazing woman.

The moment my dad releases her to me, I grip her fingers in my own. She's so soft and delicate.

Her hands are calloused from her days spent making toys in the workshop. She insists that she wants to keep making them even as we build a family. I told her I'd support all of her dreams, no matter how many children we have. I'll always have her back and always believe in her goals. I'll do everything I can to see her reach them.

The preacher is talking then. He's asking us to repeat our vows and when Cassie repeats hers, my heart nearly stops. I still can't believe she's mine. After ten years of hoping and longing, we're finally together. I wake up every morning feeling like the luckiest man on earth and go to bed every night with a smile on my face.

"You look beautiful," I whisper just before I kiss her. It's our first kiss as man and wife but the truth is, every kiss with her feels like the very first one. She was worth waiting for.

The only thing that forces me to part from my new wife is the pastor interrupting us. "Don't devour her, son."

Our friends and family chuckle. I'm crazy about this woman and I don't care who knows. It's a struggle to keep my hands to myself any time I'm around her. Micah used to get annoyed with me until he found his nanny. Now he gets it.

Ledger pats me on the back. "Don't get her pregnant right here, slugger."

"Too late for that," Micah mutters under his breath. He was at Liquid Courage when Cassie shared the news with me. He congratulated us with a big smile and told us how happy he is to be a dad.

Mom lets out a gasp.

"Fuck, sorry, Cassie," Micah apologizes before glancing toward the pastor. "Sorry for the language."

He waves it off before congratulating us.

Mom and Dad crowd around Cassie. They're so excited at the thought of welcoming another Kringle grandchild. They quickly accepted Micah's daughter and showered her with affection the moment he introduced them to her.

There's a round of hugs and congratulations and excitement before it's time to move onto the next part of the ceremony. Finally, after a long day, we're back home. Yesterday, my brothers and I moved the last of her furniture over here.

She carefully directed since I wouldn't let her lift a finger. Now that she's pregnant, I don't plan on letting her do anything.

I lock up the house and settle Snowball on her new cat tree in the living room. She climbs onto her favorite ledge and flicks her tail, studying me. I give her a scratch under the chin. "Help me watch over her now."

She meows as if pledging her protection.

The last thing I do before I head into the bedroom is set the Christmas lights on Cassie's favorite settings. They twinkle and shimmer, sure to delight her when she sees them later.

When I come into the bedroom, she's already stripped out of her dress. She's standing there in her white bra and panties. The set is far from plain though. It's been designed to look like ribbons. I'm about to lose my damn mind because my cock is so hard. "I loved the wedding dress. But I love this look even better."

"I figured it's Christmas Eve so I should get you a gift," she teases.

I prowl across the room and brush her hair from her shoulder. I press soft kisses to her skin because she loves it when I touch her here. "You've already given me the best gifts. Your heart, your body, your soul. And now, a baby."

"That one was a team project," she says as I scoop her into my arms and carry her to the bed. I spend the rest of the night giving pleasure to her curvy body and showing her all of the ways I love her.

This woman is my best friend, my wife, and my soulmate. I'll love and cherish her every day for the rest of our lives.

Want a bonus scene with West and Cassie? Sign up for my weekly newsletter and get the bonus here.

READ NEXT: A CHRISTMAS NANNY FOR THE COWBOY

Gruff cowboy seeks nanny for hire. Must love babies, flannel, and kissing under the mistletoe.

Micah

I didn't ask Santa for a baby for Christmas. But the precious bundle that was left on my doorstep needs me and I won't let her down. Problem is I can't run the Christmas tree ranch and care for a little one.

So I ask Santa to send me a nanny for Christmas who can help me with my new daughter. I just didn't expect the curvy woman who shows up for the job would be the same one I'm interested in.

But it's fine. I can treat her just like any other employee…until that kiss under the mistletoe. Could Chloe possibly be interested in a gruff older cowboy like me?

Chloe

I've had a crush on Micah Kringle for weeks now. But it's fine. I can still go to work for him as his nanny for hire. Everything is going great…until he kisses me under the mistletoe.

Now the older cowboy is growling at me and insisting I'm his. But what happens when we're done with our naughty fun? Will my filthy boss still want me, or will this holiday fling melt away to nothing?

If you're craving a sexy holiday story about a gruff cowboy who falls hard for his innocent nanny, then it's time to meet Micah in A Christmas Nanny for the Cowboy.

Read Micah and Chloe's Story

COURAGE COUNTY SERIES

Welcome to Courage County where protective alpha heroes fall for strong curvy women they love and defend. There's NO cheating and NO cliffhangers. Just a sweet, sexy HEA in each book.

Love on the Ranch

Her Alpha Cowboy

Pregnant and alone, Riley has nowhere to go until the alpha cowboy finds her. Will she fall in love with her rescuer?

Her Older Cowboy

Summer is making a baby with her brother's best friend. But he insists on making it the old-fashioned way.

Her Protector Cowboy

Jack will do whatever it takes to protect his curvy woman after their hot one-night stand…then he plans to claim her!

Her Forever Cowboy

Dean is in love with his best friend's widow. When they're stranded together for the night, will he finally tell her how he feels?

Her Dirty Cowboy

The ranch's newest hire also happens to be the woman Adam had a one-night stand with…and she's carrying his baby!

Her Sexy Cowboy

She's a scared runaway with a baby. He's determined to protect them both. But neither of them expected to fall in love.

Her Wild Cowboy

He'll keep his curvy woman safe, even if it means a marriage in name only. But what happens when he wants to make it a real marriage?

Her Wicked Cowboy

One hot night with Jake gave me the best gift of my life: a beautiful baby girl. Will he want us to be a family when I show up on his doorstep a year later?

Courage County Brides

The Cowboy's Bride

The only way out of my horrible life is to become a mail order bride. But will my new cowboy husband be willing to take a chance on love?

The Cowboy's Soulmate

Can a jaded playboy find forever with his curvy mail order bride and her baby? Or will her secret ruin their future?

The Cowboy's Valentine

I'm a grumpy loner cowboy and I like it that way. Until my beautiful mail order bride arrives and suddenly, I want more than a marriage in name only.

The Cowboy's Match

Will this mail order bride matchmaker take a chance on love when she falls for the bearded cowboy who happens to be her VIP client?

The Cowboy's Obsession

Can this stalker cowboy show the curvy schoolteacher that he's the one for her?

The Cowboy's Sweetheart

Rule #1 of becoming a mail order bride: never fall in love with your cowboy groom.

The Cowboy's Angel

Can this cowboy single dad with a baby find love with his new mail order bride?

The Cowboy's Heiress

This innocent heiress is posing as a mail order bride. But what happens when her grumpy cowboy husband discovers who she really is?

Courage County Warriors

Rescue Me

Getting out was hard. Knowing who to trust was easy: my dad's best friend. He's the only man I can count on, but will we be able to keep our hands off each other?

Protect Me

When I need a warrior to protect me, I know just who to turn to: my brother's best friend. But will this grumpy cowboy who's guarding my body break my heart?

Shield Me

When trouble comes for me, I know who to call—my ex-boyfriend's dad. He's the only one who can help. But can I convince this grumpy cowboy to finally claim me?

Courage County Fire & Rescue

The Firefighter's Curvy Nanny

As a single dad firefighter, I was only looking for a quick fling. Then the curvy woman from last night shows up. Turns out, she's my new nanny.

The Firefighter's Secret Baby

After a scorching one-night stand with a sexy firefighter, I realize I'm pregnant…with my brother's best friend's baby.

The Firefighter's Forbidden Fling

I knew a one night stand with my grumpy boss wasn't the best idea…but I didn't think it would lead to anything serious. I definitely didn't think it would lead to a surprise pregnancy with this sexy firefighter.

GET A FREE COWBOY ROMANCE

Get Her Grumpy Cowboy for FREE:
https://www.MiaBrody.com/free-cowboy/

LIKE THIS STORY?

If you enjoyed this story, please post a review about it. Share what you liked or didn't like. It may not seem like much, but reviews are so important for indie authors like me who don't have the backing of a big publishing house.

Of course, you can also share your thoughts with me via email if you'd prefer to reach out that way. My email address is mia @ miabrody.com (remove the spaces). I love hearing from my readers!

ABOUT THE AUTHOR

Mia Brody writes steamy stories about alpha men who fall in love with big, beautiful women. She loves happy endings and every couple she writes will get one!

When she's not writing, Mia is searching for the perfect slice of cheesecake and reading books by her favorite instalove authors.

Keep in touch when you sign up for her newsletter: https://www.MiaBrody.com/news. It's the fastest way to hear about her new releases so you never miss one!

Made in United States
Troutdale, OR
12/08/2023